Title: Winning Him Over
Subtitle: Billionaire and BBW MF Romance
Story
Author: Heather Berrymore

AF426755

This is a work of fiction. Any resemblance to any person, living or dead is purely coincidental.

From the Publisher:
Thank you for purchasing this book.

Table of Contents

Winning Him Over
Description

Barb is a twenty-four year old young woman who graduated from City University in her hometown about two years agao. She was an average student but it didn't bother her because she had felt that her physical assets would ultimately determine her fate.

Barb is a a big beautiful woman and any man would want to have her to himself. Owing to her attractiveness, she works steadily as a plus size model as well as being the weekend anchor on the local television station.

She had just won first place in the Miss Beautiful pageant when a man approached her. He had a purely masculine and handsome features. He was definitely striking, possessing an obvious confidence. Locking eyes, Barb noticed a sly grin upon his face and a twinkle in his. Now Barb wished more than anything she could be with him.

Chapter 1

My name is Barb Wilder. I am twenty-fours years old, and graduated two years ago from City University. I wasn't the best student. However, I felt that my physical assets would ultimately determine my fate. My family, consisting of my parents, both high-level executives for large multinational firms, and my older brother, a doctor in residence, didn't quite understand me. Yet, they didn't really nag me about academics either. I won't try to be modest in describing my body. I am a big beautiful woman, and any man would want to have me to himself. My jet-black hair extends to the middle of my back. My skin is flawlessly light-colored. Owing to my attractiveness, I work steadily as a plus size model. On the weekends, I do the news reporting on the local channel.

I had just won first place in the Miss Big and Beautiful pageant. I wasn't particularly surprised, figuring that the scores of the talent portion of the competition, in which I sang, would be heavily influenced by the impressions made by the earlier swimsuit part of the contest. Still, it was a thrill when I was announced as the winner, especially since it was over my long-time frenemy, Nan, who placed second. Nan is, I have to admit, twice as good a singer as I. However, most would consider me more physically captivating. We had been holding hands as the two finalists. When my name was announced as the winner, Nan, during the obligatory fake-hugging immediately after the announcement, had whispered in my ear, "Congratulations on your victory, Barb, but this will be the last time that you beat me in anything." She then winked at me and I couldn't tell if she was being serious or not.

While the band was still playing, a man approached me. He had a masculine handsomeness. He was wearing a fine tuxedo, which could not hide his broad shoulders and obviously muscular build. He wasn't particularly tall, being level with my height in my four-inch stiletto heels. But he was definitely striking, possessing an obvious confidence, and his eyes locked onto mine unwaveringly, a hint of a smile gracing his visage. As he drew nearer, I saw a badge that indicated that he had been one of the judges of the pageant.

"Miss Wilder, you are one very impressive woman, the whole package. I want to introduce myself. Louis Smith. I always stay tuned to the television whenever you're on and have been interested in meeting you for some time now."

"The pleasure is all mine, Mr. Smith. Please call me Barb," I purred, as I extended my hand. Louis took my hand and gave it a soft kiss. Of course, like most trendy city residents, I was familiar with the name, if not exactly the face. The gossip papers and websites had all declared him one of the regions top ten eligible bachelors ever since he returned back from Europe about eight months ago. His family was among the wealthiest in the city, with countless holdings in commercial and residential properties. He is a billionaire himself aside from his family's wealthiness. Louis, twenty-oneyears of age, had been sent six years ago in London to acquire an MBA and to cut his managerial chops by overseeing family properties in Europe. In his spare time over there, Louis co-founded an Internet start-up, which had been bought by another start-up for a hefty profit. The family had apparently called Louis back to work full-time to help manage their more extensive North American assets. The Smiths were an old-school family, very private. Even in the gossip rags, there were very few details about him and even fewer photographs of Louis' activities around the city.

"Do you know what impressed me the most about you, Barb?"

"Was it my precise pitch on the high notes?" I joked.

"Well, those were quite lovely," he chuckled. "However, I am truly impressed by your natural elegance and your big beautiful body. You exude such confidence in various situations and you carry yourself with unbelievably regal sophistication."

"Thank you, Mr. Smith. I'll still on a high from winning, so keep my high going by complimenting me more," I laughed.

"Barb, on stage there, you were a woman among girls. I would love to throw more compliments at you at a later time. Would you do me the pleasure of giving me your number? Perhaps we could have a date soon." Louis Smith then tilted his head, locked deeply into my eyes and smiled broadly, almost challenging me to try to deny his request.

"It would be my pleasure, Mr. Smith. A woman can never listen to enough compliments, especially from someone so handsome." I winked at him and then recited my number into his phone.

"Excellent, Barb! I look forward to meeting again." He headed stage right. I was then mobbed by a number of pageant officials.

As Louis Smith was about to disappear from view, I noticed that Nan had intercepted him. She was speaking to him alone. I could see her whispering into his ear at times and giggling often and playfully touching him frequently, while he seemed to have no interest in ending their conversation. After about ten minutes, however, they did go their separate ways, but not before I saw her speak into her phone.

Two hours later, after the obligatory pictures had been taken and the forms had all been signed and upcoming post-pageant meetings had been scheduled, I had finished changing into my street clothes. I was waiting for my family to take me to a small private celebration party in their apartment, when my phone rang. It was Louis Smith. "I was interested in setting up our date, Barb. Would you be free this weekend?"

I already had plans all next weekend to be away to visit with friends and attend a bachelorette party. Still, I was determined that it probably would not be wise to be unavailable for Louis Smith. I reasoned that he probably had other appealing women immediately available to him and playing hard-to-get could possibly result in never getting together. More concerning, though, was Nan's flagrant attempt at seducing him earlier and I wanted to make sure that I got to him first.

"You flatter me with your strong interest, Mr. Smith. I do have some free time this weekend. When were you thinking of?"

"All weekend, Barb. You would need to let the television station know that you will be occupied. I would like to get to know you deeply ... intimately, you might say. I've found that doing so requires an extended and concentrated amount of time together. I am quite busy and I'm used to making important decisions over short periods of time. This includes my choice of companions. I would ask that you clear your schedule from Friday evening to Monday morning. The date will continue, as long as we are getting along well. If one of us decides to terminate our date earlier in the weekend, well, I think we could both maturely go our separate ways. I see this as the best way to start learning about each other, don't you think, Barb?"

"Um, yes, you're kind of convincing, Mr. Smith. I guess I can re-arrange my schedule for you ...I mean, us."

"Call me Louis, Barb. And I understand that you may have plans already. A stunning woman like you rarely just sits at home. So, I'm offering you this. Call me on Tuesday. Tell me what you would like to do Friday evening, Saturday afternoon, Saturday evening, and Sunday afternoon. I'll make it happen. Deal?"

"Absolutely, a deal. I'm looking forward to learning about ... us, Louis."

"Great! Oh, by the way, if you wish to purchase anything for our weekend together, call my personal assistant, Jen. I'll text you her number. She can pay for many things that you may desire. In fact, I insist that you avail yourself of this offer. I'm taking up your time at the last minute and I would like to repay you in some trivial way for it. Also, if you have any requests, please convey them to her and she will see what she can do. I have to go now. Bye-bye, Barb."

"Bye, Louis. See you on Friday." The phone connection ended.

I thought about things the next day. It was quite clear that I would be expected to have a sexual relationship with Louis on Friday evening. It wasn't exactly what I wanted, as I have only had sex on a first date only once previously and it was not a particularly fond. On the other hand, I decided that I really did want to pursue this billionaire and charismatic man. If that was what he expected and the arrangement of an entire weekend date would imply this, then I determined that denying him would not further my goals. He would probably terminate the date early and would find ways to relieve his frustrations without me. So, my strategy for the weekend was to have sex early and often, but otherwise keeping him interested by being compelling in other ways—good conversation, being adventurous, demonstrating non-sexual talents. I found it weird that key elements of our rendezvous were quite unconventional. The man had proposed a first date, but I was the one scheduling activities and sexual intercourse was already presumed.

I called Jen on Monday. "Yes, Miss Wilder. Mr. Smith told me you might call," she said, after I had introduced myself. "How may I help you?"

"Louis mentioned that if I wanted to purchase some items, that I should call you. Is that right? If so, I may be buying some clothes and accessories. Would that be too presumptuous?"

She replied curtly, "No, of course not. Mr. Smith is very generous with money, but he does have high standards, so do go for quality, Ms. Wilder. That is my advice to you. I figure that if you keep the costs under seventy-five thousand dollars, that would be absolutely fine. By the way, don't buy any jewelry. Two reasons, the first is that every item bought will technically be his, so you can't presume to keep any jewelry. Second, he will probably buy you a necklace anyway this weekend. Anything else, Ms. Wilder?"

"Oh yes. I would like to see if I could come over to Louis' residence Friday morning. I decided that for Friday evening, we could just have a private dinner at his place. I wanted to prepare myself for the evening over there."

"I would need to check with Mr. Smith, but I suspect that would be fine. I'll let you know the next time you call and I helping you finalize purchases."

I got to work. I had only a couple of short photo shoots and a few meals with my family and friends scheduled for the week. So I had plenty of time to plan for what I considered to be a very important weekend.

After working out at the gym and getting a French manicure, I arrived mid-morning at Louis' lavish four-bedroom penthouse in the Golden Mile district. Jen met me at the door. I was slightly surprised by her appearance, as I had expected someone much older. Jen seemed to be roughly my age and was quite attractive in her white short pencil-skirt suit with matching high-heeled pumps; I wondered if there was a backstory to her employment with Louis. She showed me into a large guestroom with its own bathroom. After a very business-like tour of the penthouse, Jen left. I unpacked my clothes and placed them inside the walk-in closet and took a bath.

At noon, a chef arrived, also young and remarkably attractive, although her figure was largely hidden by her frumpy work attire. She introduced herself as Carina and made me a noodle dish for lunch. She then began preparing a dinner for two. While she was making dinner, the hairstylist from the studio came up, a personal favor to me. He gaped at the opulence of the apartment and told me that it would seem that he would have to do some of his most fabulous work with me today. He did, leaving me with a magnificent, voluminous updo that left my neck tastefully bare and a few tendrils of hair framing my face. The look appeared both innocent and sophisticated. Both my hairstylist and the cook left mid-afternoon, which left me with a few hours before Louis would come back.

I started by having a clean shave to make my skin feel sexy smooth. I did leave a small rectangular landing strip around my vagina. I figured that I could invite Louis to remove that later, if he so wanted. I spent over an hour doing my eyes, just to ensure that my lashes were thick and long, my brows were shaped and penciled flawlessly, and that the light bronze eye shadow with just a touch of shimmer gave off the right look. I applied a hint of pink blush to highlight my cheekbones. I sprayed perfume on my neck, wrists, breast cleavage, and inner thighs.

Then I dressed. I had spent only half of the budget limit on my outfits for the days with Louis and I was certain that it would pay off. I slipped on a black thong which barely covered my landing strip. It certainlycouldn't quite cover my puffy pussy lips, and turned into floss on the backside. It wasn't really serving any real functional purpose, but I knew that either Louis or I could have fun with it. My little black dress was a clingy silk cowled halter. The cowl plunged past my chest and was adorned at its bottom near my navel with a diamond-jeweled medallion. The inner halves of my large and firm breasts were fully displayed.

The cut of the dress left the side of my breasts visible and my entire back naked down to the crack of my ass. The design of the dress did not permit a bra, thus the points of my nipples were vaguely visible through the fabric. The hem, being six inches above the knee, gave the illusion of being slightly more conservative, but there was a long slit along the right side that ended level with my "kitty." I had bought a befitting size model, smaller than my usual size, so the dress was skin tight, with the result that a deep cleavage was created and that my ass and thighs appeared to be simply painted black.

Even so, I had selected the dress well. It was obviously well-cut and designed, showing sophistication and quality, so that the initial impression would be elegance rather than slutty.

I fastened on my shoes. They were black Manolo Blahnik sandals with two-inch platforms, each with a single half-inch front strap that ran across the slightly behind the toes and a buckled criss-crossing ankle strap around the back. Each sandal had a six-inch gold metallic stiletto heel and my slender and shapely legs looked fantastic with that elevation. I had carefully chosen the dimensions of my footwear. Wearing these shoes would leave probably leave me a few inches taller than Louis in his bare feet, but lengthening the appearance of my legs was just the impression I wanted. And like my dress, the shoes were a size too small and left the tips of my toes just slightly overhanging the platform, which previous lovers had found to be advantageous when sucking on my toes. These sandals were clearly FMS, fuck-me shoes, although I didn't need the shoes to declare my intent, considering the design of my LBD.

I heard the front door open. Louis' voice shouted, "Barb, are you here? I'm back a little early. Couldn't wait to see you. But finish up what you are doing. I'll get us a couple of drinks. Meet me in the living room."

"What a pleasant surprise to have you back so early, Louis. I'll just be another fifteen minutes. It'll be worth the slight wait, though," I replied loudly from the guestroom. I put on two-inch gold hoop earrings and a thin jade bracelet onto my left wrist. Jen had hinted that Louis might present me with a necklace, so I didn't wear one of my own. I looked at myself in a full-length mirror, giggling like a schoolgirl. I had achieved the exact effect I wanted. Angel from the neck up, devil from the neck down. Louis would be torn between trying to protect my innocence or trying to ravage my sinful body. Of course, the latter would win out, as it always does. I debated for a while and decided to tip the scales a bit more. I penciled around my naturally full lips, slightly puckered on the top and engorged on the bottom, ones that countless people assume are injected with collagen.

Then I applied bright red glossy lipstick over them, a clear invitation to intimacy, as if more hints were actually needed. Then I walked out of the guestroom.

Chapter 2

"Having you here, Barb, already makes it a great weekend." My arms were still wrapped around his neck, so Louis spoke with his lips just a few inches from mine.

"You promised me compliments for this date, cutie. Would you like to be more specific? Is it the possibility of listening to some of my great jokes? Or maybe my potential to advise you on some important business decisions?" I teased. Locking in on his eyes, I grazed his cock with the back of my right hand. I softly and suggestively said, "Would you like me to take a wild guess? Does it have anything to do with realizing what kind of fun you'll have eyeing me and playing with me for the next few days?"

Louis spoke in a controlled voice, at least initially. "Well, you are very mesmerizing, Barb. You are gorgeous and have a spectacular body. And you obviously spent significant time preparing yourself. Your make-up and hair, your flawless skin, your attire, so elegantly sensual. I'm not sure what I should do, maybe you could advise me. I want to take things slowly right now, to get to know the person behind that sweet innocent face.

"Such graceful lines, soulful eyes, cute nose, full lips. But I can't help myself, I am so drawn to you sexually. But your figure, your body, those huge breasts, that round ass, those long-toned legs, you have such a fuckable body, excuse my language ... ", he babbled, his words finally betraying his initial attempt at reigning in his libido.

"Do go on. I love that language," I whispered seductively.

"... I don't know whether to lose myself in a long kiss with you or to fuck ... fuck you raw." He panted the last phrase out.

"Maybe both, dear. But let's start with a kiss and see where that takes us. Oh, and please remember that this is the only outfit I have for dinner tonight, cutie," I said with deliberately confounding cheeriness. I tilted his head slightly and planted my lips directly on his, giving him a little peck.

His response was ravenous. He urgently engaged my lips and left them there. His hands wrapped around my backside and they began to determinedly explore and massage my back and butt. I felt his tongue lightly touching mine and I returned more firmly in kind. He then began exploring my mouth and I his. After about ten minutes of this, all in silence, Louis pulled from the kissing, but kept his hands around my ass. He lustily stared at my eyes for a good minute, as if trying to make up his mind about something.

He then dragged me down onto the plush carpet, in between the sofa and a large low-lying glass table, hands still on my ass, with him on the bottom. Then he resumed exploring my mouth with his tongue and massaging my back and ass with one hand and steadying my head with the other, all-in silence. After about five minutes, he again stopped and wordlessly stared into my eyes. For fun, I gave him my patented pouty cute look.

"Don't give me that, you slut," he muttered. He rolled me over. He unhurriedly and gently kissed my neck and I arched it high for him. He must have pecked at my neck at least twenty times, but the last one was a fiercely focused one that would certainly leave a hickey later. His entire body descended lower and lower, hands along my sides and legs, tenderly kissing his way down. My pussy, already moist from earlier, began to leak in response to his persistent oral attention to my body. I moved my right arm from the floor, placed it through the side slit of the skirt, and onto my clit.

Then I felt my breasts being kissed and licked, slowly and softly, one then the other, with agonizing patience, but without ever getting to my covered nipples. I might have climaxed right then, had he decided to suck on them. But he didn't, despite having his lips on my breasts for over five minutes. I couldn't take it anymore and wildly rubbed my clit with one hand and pressed on my mound with the other, desperately trying to achieve orgasm, as more juices leaked and soaked my sorry excuse for knickers. Then he surprised me by leaving my breasts, continuing to kiss down my belly until finally circling his tongue endlessly around my navel. As I continued to teeter at the edge, he whispered, "Clever girl, exposing so much skin in the front. I love tasting you, Barb. Now, can I help you down there?" I just moaned, breathing shallowly and rapidly.

He placed two fingers inside me. After just two strokes into my pussy, I convulsed violently and screamed, "FUUUUUCK MEEEEEE!" I began repeating, "Oh my God, Oh my God, Oh my God ...", as he metronomically went in and out at a sluggish pace. My whole body writhed and both hands gripped his shoulders in an attempt to get him to stop, the sensation becoming too intense. But he just steadily kept on stroking inside, while now using his other hand to furiously rub my clit, until I finally went limp and changed my orgasmic Whimpering, I said, "Please stop, please stop. I'll do anything for you, if you stop."

He stopped. After a bit, he growled menacingly, "Just what I was waiting to hear, my whore. Get on your knees." I slowly managed to get on all fours. He sat down on the couch. He resumed, flatly stating, "You know what to do."

I took my time unzipping his fly. By now, my head had cleared. He had no underwear on. I pulled out his circumcised cock, which was mostly hard. I was not particularly skilled with fellatio, having not had much practice until only more recently; fellatio is fundamentally a submissive act and I was used to the majority of my previous lovers trying to please me than the other way around. Still, I knew the basics. I made sure he saw me lick my lips and kiss the tip of his cock a number of times, all while gazing at him submissively. I languidly circled the head over and over, eyes still in upgaze, pausing to lick the frenulum and the meatus each time. With each lick, I noticed Louis shuddered a bit. His cock was fully rigid now, a penis I estimated at about six inches and a bit more than an inch in diameter. I was glad at its normal dimensions, as I had never noticed a correlation between size and my personal pleasure and I hated the potential prospect of deep-throating something too big.

I broke off my gaze and concentrated on his member. Moving my head back and forth, I progressively enveloped the first three inches of his cock. My right hand jerked off the back half, with the long-manicured nails of my left-hand tickling underneath his scrotum. I made some non-specific cooing noises while slurping him. Louis wordlessly scanned what he could see of my body, certainly admiring my delicate neck, my toned back, my well-defined calves. At some point, I got the sense he was willing himself to ejaculate. "Keep it up, Barb. This blowjob feels so good. I wish this could go on forever. You are so talented. You have such a talented mouth. What a talented cock-sucker." He continued with variations of these phrases, all while closing his eyes.

I suspected that he was only rambling in order to drive himself to orgasm. Sure enough, within a minute, his penis jerked and I felt a small spurt in my mouth. I instantly pulled out and rapidly pumped his manhood with my hand, most of his cum landing on my neck and my chest, some of it staining the cowl of my dress. Even when he ran dry, I continued to pump, until finally his cock began to go flaccid.

I got up and cleaned both of us up with some tissue found on the glass table behind me. Louis simply stayed seated, eyes closed, with his head extended backward against the top of the sofa. When he finally opened his eyes to look at me, I mouthed, "Thank you."

He nodded. "No, thank YOU. You are so sexy, Barb. Your lips are so amazing around my mouth and around my cock. So incredibly full and so sensual."

"You are so kind. They are quite inviting, aren't they?" I agreed, puckering them a few times. My eyes twinkled as I continued, "Oops, you didn't mean down there, did you?"

Louis laughed. "I don't know yet. Maybe I'll get to find out later." He paused and looked at me yearningly. "I can't get over how responsive your body is, Barb. I can only imagine how it will react when we are nude together, making love tonight."

"Don't get ahead of yourself, sweetie. I am a conservative girl. What makes you think that'll happen?" I teased, a big smirk on my face.

"Because I'm going to treat you like a princess for the rest of the evening. You won't be able to resist my charms and you'll beg me to sleep with you tonight," he said with a touch of arrogance.

I decided to have fun with him. "The way I see it, dear, you won't be able to resist my sexy body, which I'll flaunt all evening until YOU beg to ravage me tonight."

Louis stood up, picked up two filled stemmed glasses from the center of the table and handed me one. "This champagne is probably flat by now. I poured it over an hour ago. Still, let's toast. To Barb, best wishes for winning her challenge."

"And to Louis," I followed. "Best wishes for winning his challenge." We intertwined our right arms and drained the flat champagne. I gave him a peck on his mouth. "Thank you for inviting me for the weekend. You're right, it will be a great weekend."

"You're welcome, Barb. The pleasure is all mine. Foreplay is now over, though. Time for the main course."

"What?" I exclaimed. "We each just had an orgasm. You have stamina for more?"

"I have stamina like you wouldn't believe, Miss Wilder. But, silly you. Did you think I meant another round of sex? All this physical activity has made me hungry and I believe Carina made us a delicious three-course meal." He extended his hand.

I could only laugh, as I took his hand and walked to the dining room.

It was a fine dinner. The nighttime view of city from his penthouse was magnificent. As were the food and the conversation, both enhanced by a bottle of vintage white wine that Louis told me he had had from before he left for London and was saving for a special occasion. He was a perfect gentleman, seated across from me in the middle of a long glass table meant for six. He listened attentively to what I had to say and was forthcoming with his own thoughts. For the most part, he focused on my eyes during our almost non-stop conversation, occasionally touching my arms or hands, generally undistracted my subtle and unsubtle attempts to display various features of my body.

Subtle, like often leaning my chest forward and frequently adjusting the halter straps around my chest.

Unsubtle, like when I unbuckled my right stilletos, exposed my entire toned thigh through the slit of my dress, and slid my foot up his pant leg. I got the reaction I wanted for that trick, as Louis simply stared wide-eyed through the table and re-adjusted his pants to accommodate a growing bulge in his crotch. When he finally looked up, I simply winked at him and licked my lips with a grin.

Chapter 3

Despite my little teases, we did learn about each other. Louis told me stories about his activities in Britain and all over Europe. He told me that it was actually his idea to go there, finally convincing his family when he when he was accepted to university, and after he promised to manage and help grow the various family holdings in London and across Europe while there. He described how he and two friends from school worked long hours developing a real-estate website, building a real-world infrastructure around it, marketing it, watching it modestly take off, and finally negotiating a lucrative buyout. "That was the best thing I have ever done, Barb, not just the sale, but the process. I did it myself, minimal help from my family. Although, let's face it, not to take too much credit, I never had to worry about running out of funds for myself and some aspects were easier because of family connections and intuition honed by being around the family business. But what can I do, Barb, I am a child of my circumstances and I can't just pretend it doesn't exist, you know?"

"There must have been a lot of personal adjustments you had to make coming back here."

"A few. I'm a bit less dependent on help. I drive my own car. I do have people on my payroll, though, like my cook and my maid, both great finds. You probably already met my cook Carina, who is really talented at nourishing me, I think. She comes about three times a week. You won't be meeting my housekeeper Irene, though. She works here every day quietly before the sun even rises and many mid-afternoons when I'm at work. Mostly I see her when I can't sleep."

"Your assistant appears quite professional, too. I've had a number of conversations with her this week and met her earlier today."

Louis chuckled. "Jen. Jen is quite a revelation. My life would be significantly more frustrating without her. She is quite discreet and expertly satisfies all the crazy desires that I request of her." Louis then paused, ruminating over what he just said. "Just so you know, there's nothing personal between us, though. She is a complete professional, as you just noted, Barb."

I revealed to Louis I wanted to work more in the television or movie industry, not necessarily as an actress, but more on the production side. I wanted to be part of the creative process, both artistic and business, that existed on the other side of the camera. And I confided that I wanted to still be important when my beauty eventually faded. I didn't know whether he believed me or not. I'm not sure I would believe it, if someone like me said that. But it's the truth and t's the reason I regret the way I passed through higher education. I told him I entered the Miss Big and Beautiful pageant because I was hoping it could be my passport to the industry, obviously as an actress, even though I doubted I had acting talent and had only rudimentary training. I aspired to one day parlay acting gigs into writing or directing or producing. "I really pray that I get the chance one day to show the people who makes the shows that I am more than a pretty face ... and a body that powerful men would beg on their knees to fuck, of course." I added the last phrase with a grin. "Speaking of fuck, Louis, something just occurred to me."

"What would that be?"

"You know how you said you didn't know whether to lose yourself in a kiss with me or fuck me raw? You pretty much only did the first one."

"I know. It was what I felt most strongly at the time and I think it was the right choice. Don't you agree?"

"Don't you think you deserve more, sweetie?"

"Barb, don't trick me to win a bet," he replied, with a hearty laugh. "By the way, it's now ten o'clock. Do you still want to go out dancing?"

"Absolutely. I want to show off my killer moves for you, dear."

"Great! Do you think you can get ready in ten minutes? My housekeeper will clean all this up. Oh, and please just wear what you have on now, Barb, if that would be acceptable to you. I love your look. You have such great taste. By the way, what is your neck size?"

I told him and we walked to our separate rooms. I touched up my make-up, brushed my teeth and rinsed my mouth, and spritzed a touch more perfume. I went to the front door, waiting. Louis, now dressed in a stylish double-breasted dark suit, came out with a small box. He opened it, revealing a silver choker with a single row of diamonds.

"Thank you for clearing your schedule for me, Barb. Do you like it?"

"I love it, Louis!" I squealed.

"I bought three of the same style actually since I didn't know your size. My assistant will return the other two on Monday. May I put in on?"

"Of course. Don't let me distract you." I came in closer, pressing against his body, and kissed him on the right cheek, leaving a bright red impression on his face. Then I did the same to his right shirt collar, which also exposed the back of my neck. Louis took this opportunity to fasten the choker.

"Shall we?" Louis held my hand, as we walked out the door.

As we waited for the elevator, I said to him, "Just a warning. Don't wash off the lipstick from your face or your shirt until we get back. I want everyone to know you are mine, you are MY property. It's only fair anyway, with that big hickey you left on my neck from before dinner." He squeezed my hand lovingly, but did not actually look that amused.

I was told the dance club was about fifteen minutes away in the nighttime traffic. Louis drove a black Ferrari convertible and decided to leave the top open. It was hard to talk. So I took the opportunity to wet his appetite. I softly massaged his left thigh, ever so close to his obviously rigid cock, for much of the trip. I pulled out lipstick from my small clutch twice, so he could watch me apply it from the corner of his eye. At one point, without him noticing, I untied and tied back my halter, slipping the trailing part of the seat belt underneath it. And I exposed all of my right leg the entire ride. I made sure he noticed me deliberately admiring it and continuously running my hand across its length. When the club came into view, I asked him to stop.

"What's wrong?" he asked, pulling over.

"My panties are bothering me. They were soaked with my juices before dinner and they never dried out because my pussy has been constantly wet ever since." This last part was not really true, but what's wrong a little white lie anyway? "I need to take it off." I then slowly wiggled off the the damp piece of floss. "Just as I thought, quite moist. Would you be a dear and hold them for me in your coat?" I paused to sniff it before handing them over to Louis.

Louis shook his head, grinned, and put them in his breast pocket, as if it were a pocket square. He then drove over to the valet. I stayed in my seat, even after an attendant opened my door. Louis came over to my side, tipped the passenger side valet, and indicated he would take over. "Sweetie, I seem to have a problem here. Somehow the seat belt has tangled with my dress. Could you help me out?"

Louis looked closely and laughed. "Naughty girl," he said. "May I?" He began to pull the halter knot.

"Be careful. You wouldn't want my girls to pop out now, would you? God knows they want to, with them being so big and this dress being so confining," I said playfully.

"I'll take care to defend your honor, Barb ... at least for right now."

He untangled me. I then swung my legs out, making sure both were exposed up to the upper thighs. I slowly placed my right, then my left, fuck-me shoes on the ground, making sure Louis got a extended eyeful. I do have attractive legs. They are long and smooth, none of which I take particular credit for. They are also very toned and shapely, which I do take credit for, a product of extensive work at the gym; like most of my body, there is just enough fat to smooth out excessive muscle definition, but when I flex, the individual muscle groups come nicely into view. I winked at him before finally taking his hand to emerge from the deep bucket seat of the car.

We evidently had an approved reservation. After Louis talked to the doorman, we were brought through the front door by a host, cutting in front of a line that stretched half a block, populated with many women in tight skirts barely covering their ass. The host led us to the back and seated us at a dimly lighted private booth for two with a heavy wrap-around curtain. The club itself was full but not packed, with about a couple arms-length distance between guests. The centrally-located dance floor was slightly more packed. Moderately loud house music seemed to be the dominant musical style and conversing would require either a very loud voice or close proximity. A hostess came over shortly with two stem glasses and opened bottle of Dom Perignon for us. Louis and I downed a glass before I grabbed his hand and I whispered in his ear, "Come with me."

I am a fantastic dancer. I have taken lessons since youth for all types of dance and I have spent too many nights in dance clubs for me not to be in total control on the floor. Louis was both capable enough to keep up and savvy enough to just let me do my thing. For my part, when not touching him, I made sure to constantly maintain frequent eye and bodily contact. I occasionally held both his hands to pull him near me, while I writhed. And, of course, I frequently turned my back to him to grind my ass on his bulging crotch, while directing his hands to wrap around my pelvic region.

We returned back to our seats after about twenty minutes of this, just before developing any sweat. We people-watched for quite a while, having fun pointing out things to each other, laughing at some of the bad dancing and aborted pick-up attempts.

Eventually, Louis draped his left arm over my shoulder and I nestled my head on his chest, my right arm wrapped around his back and my left hand absent-mindedly groping between his legs. We sat silently, uninterested in speaking, secure in the current state of our relationship. After a while, I closed the curtain around our booth. In the privacy of our little world, I sat on his lap sideways and we began to kiss deeply, my hands on his head and his around my torso. I became increasingly excited and my bare pussy was starting to leak. Our lips still locked, I pushed him back onto the seat, so that he was underneath me. Louis was initially motionless, while I rapidly drove my hips up and down onto his crotch, trying to relieve my tension. I began to moan with greater desperation and Louis started to buck his hips a bit. "Help me, help me ... " I mouthed repeatedly.

Then, all of a sudden, my left arm hit the champagne bottle and it shattered on the floor, the sound loudly piercing through the music. The moment was ruined. I sat up and straightened up my dress. "I got a little carried away, sweetie. Sorry."

Attendants opened the curtain and fussed over us, trying to remove the glass and mop up the liquid. People were staring at us and the commotion around us. I decided to use the time to continue placing my lips all over Louis' face, marking my man for all to see. Louis, however, did not reciprocate my attention to him. Instead, he sat rather stiffly and tried to distance himself a bit. Sensing his unease, I stopped kissing him and apologized.

"Barb, nothing to be sorry about. Maybe we should leave, though. It's not a particularly private place here, anyway." I found it difficult, given my confidence in my ability to inspire lust in men, to believe that his interest in me was waning this early.

Perhaps, he was playing the game that lovers play when they are unsure of the other's true feelings, a defense mechanism. Taking it slow to make sure your interest will not be unrequited. I didn't know him well enough to know for sure what he was thinking, though. All I knew was that I was feeling possessive right now. I wanted his body and soul committed to me right now and I wanted to show it.

"I agree, cutie. Let's go back to your place. Maybe we can have fun there. Shall we use facilities before we leave?"

We both left our seats. I took longer in the bathroom, of course. When I emerged, I could see that Louis had already returned to the booth. I decided to make him a touch jealous in the remaining time left in the club. Trolling, I call it. Far from the booth, but clearly in Louis' line of sight, I pretended to be lost, standing alone. As expected, when a pretty woman with tits the size of grapefruits, a bubble-butt ass, slender legs that appear to stretch forever, and dressed to show off all of those assets stands alone by herself, a phenomenon like air rushing into a vacuum occurs. A tall and handsome man approached me, complimenting me on my general beauty and, oh, could he buy me a drink or would I like to dance? I flirted with him for a minute, adjusting my dress, telling him how attractive he was, laughing a bit, touching his forearm, and finally lied to him that I was with friends.

He offered his card and I placed it in my clutch. I walked somewhere else and, of course, a similar encounter repeated itself. After four of these encounters, I quit trolling and walked back to the booth.

Louis appeared a bit annoyed. "Ready to go?" he asked a bit brusquely.

"Sure, dear," I replied cheerfully, although I was actually a bit worried about how Louis perceived my little adventure just now.

We rode back in silence, even though the top of the convertible was now closed because of the coolness of the midnight air. I spent the drive massaging his neck, while he left both hands on the steering wheel. After parking the car, we went up the elevator, and entered his flat. Louis escorted me to my guestroom and turned on the lights for me. "It's been a long night, Barb. Thank you for the evening. I believe we still have some nice activities tomorrow, right?" he said in a subdued voice.

"I am definitely looking forward to tomorrow, Louis." I felt that somehow the budding relationship was taking a step backward. I was determined to end tonight moving forward. "Would you like to come in? I could really use some help. You know, these shoes, they are really not meant for dancing and, well, my feet are hurting. Would you mind trying to make them feel better?"

"That will be fine, Barb. I appreciated your choice of heels tonight and the sacrifices you may have made to wear them. They brought out the best in your fantastic legs. And they really did display your your pretty feet well." He caressed my right leg with the back of his hand and furtively glanced at my feet.

I sensed a thaw. "I didn't realize you found my feet pretty, dear. Do you have a little foot and shoe fetish? Tell me what you like about them, sweetie," I teased. I sat down on the bed, crossed my right leg, and began to touch my right foot.

"I prefer to think of it as an admiration." Louis kneeled on the floor, gripping my knees and staring downwards. "The thin spike heels just scream of sex, Barb, how else am I supposed to think about them? I admire the way the ankle straps of your sandals draw me into the exquisite features of your delicate ankles ... " I caressed my right ankle. "... and how the sole design shows off your very high arches ..." I then caressed my arch. "... and how the thin front strap just highlights and exposes your beautiful toes, so well-manicured, so absolutely cute dangling a bit over your platforms, so succulent, so inviting ..." Louis seemed to be going into a trance now, obviously associating my shoes and feet with sexual urges.

"You know, my toes are a little cold right now." I wiggled my right toes. "They could use some warming up," I whispered invitingly.

Louis didn't need more encouragement to take the bait. He instantly grabbed my right sandal with both hands and placed my right big toe in his mouth. His tongue greedily licked all around it. After about a minute, he released it with a soft kiss at the end and proceeded to move onto the adjacent toe. I watched him as he did this for each toe on my right foot. Louis looked up at this point, expectantly. I nodded, reading his thoughts.

He immediately dropped to his head further, while grabbing my left sandal and lifting my entire left leg up, so that he could resume on my left toes. I wasn't sure if I wasn't becoming more aroused than he evidently was. I was witnessing this powerful man groveling at my feet, hungry to devour them. I closed my eyes as he started with my left big toe. I stayed in the moment, feeling the moistness of his mouth suck and lick the remaining toes and sensing my pussy leaking again.

He finished with my toes and then pushed my torso from an upright seated position to a supine position upon the bed. Still kneeling, he swung both my legs onto the bed and began kissing and licking my ankles. I couldn't take it anymore and I brought my right hand over to rub my clit. After a bit, I started gasping, making small mewing sounds. I shuddered, a small orgasm sweeping over me. In crazy desperation, I used my other hand to untie the halter of my dress, pushed aside the cups hiding my areola, and commenced rubbing my right nipple.

Louis noticed. With my remaining rational brain cells, I recognized a look I had seen many times before. He was absolutely lusting over my large pillowy-soft tits, which were now shaking and heaving with my rapid gasps. With a crazed desperation equal to mine, he panted, "I need your body now, Barb. I really, really need it. Please give it to me ..."

I just nodded with small quick head movements, eyes and mouth wide open, fingers still rubbing my clit, as I yelled, "I'M CUMINNNNNNG! Oh my God, oh my God ..."

Chapter 4

Louis then quickly launched his head from my feet to my left breast, cupping the mound with both hands, attacking the nipple with his lips, his saliva dripping all over the mammary. At this point, my legs had come together and he ground his crotch against them, apparently trying to find something to stimulate his stiffy. In the dying moments of my orgasm, I unbuckled his pants, opened the fly and pushed the garment to his knees.

I stroked his manhood as best I could with my right hand and tried to stabilize his body by wrapping my left arm around his back, but he continued to wildly grind his hips against me. When my left breast became extremely slippery from saliva, he switched over to sucking and slurping the right nipple, while continuing to fondle the left breast.

My right hand could feel pre-cum starting to drip from his penis. With the extra lubrication, my stroking became more regular. I slowly went up and down the entire shaft with my hand. Louis stopped moving his hips, his manhood sufficiently stimulated. I responded by gripping the head and rubbing his head rhythmically with my thumb, resulting in a notable twitching of his legs. He continued to play with my boobs, eventually smearing copious amounts of saliva over the surface of both of them.

Louis suddenly twisted away from my grip. He moved himself toward my head and went from prone on my body to straddling his legs around my abdomen. He placed his iron-hard rod between my tits and pushed them together. I quickly understood and replaced his hands with mine, while he placed his hands on the bed, next to my head. He spasmodically rocked his hips a couple of times. Groaning, he ejaculated thick white streams of cum, hitting and dribbling off my forehead, my mouth, my chin, my neck. He was probably spent, but I continued to encourage him to fuck my tits. "Baby, give me some more, give your lover some more ..." After jerking himself off between my chest pillows a few more times, he collapsed onto me.

It was a nice feeling having him on top of me. I managed to slide upward a bit.

While Louis lay exhausted on me, I gave him soft kisses all around his face. After a bit, Louis stirred. He returned my kisses, softly, one for one, and, in due course, we finally settled on a prolonged kiss on the lips, our tongues dancing and our arms wrapped around each other. It was my first prolonged post-sex embrace with him, one that I have never forgotten even to this day. My endorphins were running high and I was in heaven.

I unclinched first. "Louis, dear, may I sleep with you tonight? I really need to. Please, honey, I desperately need to be next to you, to feel you, to see you, to hear you," I whispered, inches from his face, locking in on his eyes.

"Of course. I would like that, too. I am so fond of you, Barb. Not just your sexy body. You. All of you. You should know that, Barb."

"Thank you," I murmured, casting my eyes downward.

"Barb, I don't think 'thank you' is the right response, but you're welcome. Now, how long will you need before you meet me in the master bedroom?" He rolled off my body, still lying on the bed.

"About an hour, maybe? It'll be worth the wait. I'll make sure that you find me pleasing, my sweetie. Oh, and one other thing ..." I got off the bed and, smiling at Louis, pulled my dress down to my feet. I leisurely walked around the room, pretending to tidy things up, nude in heels, careful to place one foot directly in front of the other, in order to maximize the wiggle of my ass and the jiggle in my boobs. I bent over a couple times, legs straight, pretending to pick up some stray lint, my ass and sex directly pointing at him each time. Then I walked into the bathroom.

I quickly showered, leaving the semen-encrusted choker on, and washed my face. The sticky cum on my upper body, as well as my own sticky juices around my inner thighs, were washed off. I brushed my teeth and gargled with mouthwash. I dried off the choker. I spritzed a bit of perfume on my neck, behind my ears, and on my wrists.

I put on a matching lingerie set. I had done a photo shoot about a year ago with this exact set and the company had let me keep it. I had been waiting for the right time to wear it and now was the right time. The outfit was pale pink and sheer, hiding nothing.

The first piece was a lace baby doll with a hem to just above my crotch and held up by thin shoulder straps, designed with a deep V-neck, a thin satin under bust strap accented with a long central bow, and a flyaway back. I was proud how my full and firm boobs remained high on my chest, despite being unsupported, and how well the cups of the baby doll highlighted my areolas and enticingly prominent nipples. The second piece was a lace garter that narrowed in the back to afford a full view of the entirety of my toned round butt. I placed a crotchless pair of panties, which consisted of a mesh front panel that just barely covered over my tiny landing strip and floss-thin material everywhere else. The panties required much patience to put on appropriately, as they were secured to the hips by delicate ties on each side, in order to facilitate removal. I giggled at how much time it had taken to tie on the piece, knowing how quickly it would fall off. I then rolled up a back-seamed lace-top stocking up each leg. As I fastened each garter strap, I couldn't help but think how smooth the stockings felt on me.

The final piece of the set was a floor-length sheer silk gown, with wide long butterfly sleeves, white trim, and a thin white silk front tie.

I saw my reflection in the full-length mirror. I knew the effect of the ensemble would be devastating. The pretty lingerie set, while pretending to defend my innocence and modesty, was essentially a transparent wrapping that seductively brought attention to and inviting inspection of each part of my young, supple, flawless body. The whole thing was a like fantasy bridal set, except in pink.

Excited and confident, I reapplied make-up. I decided to continue to emphasize a demure look. My hair was still in an updo and I left it alone. I lengthened my lashes with copious mascara, applied neutral eye shadow with a matte finish, and used very little eye liner. I brushed on a heavy amount of pink blush around my cheeks. I outlined my lips and applied glossy pale pink lipstick. Then I put on the choker back on and a pair of dangling single-stoned diamond earrings. Finally, I slipped on my sandals. They were a pink pair that I had spent countless hours looking for this past week, trying to find something that best matched the exact shade of pink of the lingerie set. The front of each sandal had a single set of three crisscrossing straps with a cute rose detail centrally where the straps crossed; the back of the sandal was a simple yet graceful unbuckled slingback; the sole was flat to the ground and the stiletto heel was only 3 inches in height. I grinned, sure that Louis would have plenty to "admire" with my choice of footwear. It oozed sensuality and showed off my delicate ankles, high arches, and succulent toes to full effect, while keeping my standing height such that I would not tower over him in my attempt to convey a submissive role.

I exited the guestroom and crossed past the dining and living rooms to arrive at the master bedroom. I knocked on the half-closed door. "May I come in?"

"Just wait." Through the crack in the door, I watched Louis get off the fully made bed, walk to the other side to fold over the near corner of the top sheets of the bed, and dim the lights. He was dressed just in a black silk boxer short. Despite already having had two orgasms each, I had not seen his nearly naked body. I was not disappointed. He had large and defined muscles everywhere, with very little excess fat. He had impressively large pecs and arms, a narrow waist with a hint of a six-pack abdomen, and thick thighs. I was going to enjoy being nude in bed with him, touching and being securely held by that magnificent physique. My pussy was already becoming wet in anticipation.

I entered and he gasped sharply. I decided to play out the moment, to establish my submissive role. I cast my head and eyes slightly downward and asked, "Do I please you, sweetie? Am I pretty enough for you to sleep next to you in bed tonight, honey?"

Louis circled behind me. He wrapped his muscular arms around my waist and whispered in my ear, "You look so divinely beautiful, Miss Wilder. It would be my pleasure to share my bed with you tonight. Would you consider sleeping with me nude, though? It would be much more intimate, don't you agree?"

Still facing away from him, I softly replied, "Would you like to undress me, sweetie? I would prefer that you unwrap your present yourself. Be gentle, please. I am feeling quite vulnerable." That last phrase came out of my mouth as a line for the role I was trying to project, But as I heard it spoken, I realized it was true. I actually was feeling vulnerable, with this powerful man starting to peel away not just my lingerie, but also my emotional defenses.

"Barb, please trust me. I will be gentle with you. Your heart is safe with me. I will worship you."

Hearing this, my pussy started to leak yet again tonight.

"Naughty girl. I can see all of you inside the exquisite wrapping of yours." Louis untied the gown and slipped it off my shoulders. As the gown floated down to the white carpet, he tenderly kissed my neck a couple times before working his kisses down my back and kneeling. I moaned quietly. He deftly untied the side straps of my wet knickers, which, in its dampness, dropped quickly between my feet. He moved away. "Turn around and step forward a little," he commanded.

I complied. He had positioned himself about two meters away, eyeing me yearningly. "Your sex is so pretty, Barb, so well-manicured, the lips so sensual and inviting. May I enter inside tonight?"

"I'm so wet down there ..." I knew it was a silly reply to blurt out, but my mind was fogging up with lust and I could only come up with that primal response. I could feel liquid oozing down my thighs.

Louis unhurriedly advanced toward me. His strong arms encircled my waist from the front and he gave me a soft kiss on my lips. "Patience, patience, my dear," he murmured. He then untied the back of the babydoll and pushed the straps off my shoulders. The piece floated to the floor. I was now just wearing only a garter belt, stockings, and sandals.

Louis stepped back again. "Your figure is so perfect, Barb. I'll bet you are so proud to possess such large and firm breasts ... and with such nice long and erect nipples to boot. And your tummy, so flat and defined. Barb, I would like to ask a favor. Will you press your bosom against me tonight? Will you let me explore the curves of your belly tonight?" I could only manage to make an unintelligible squeak. "I would like you to remove your belt now," he ordered. Almost mad by carnal passion, I fumbled to unclip the thin satin garters from the stockings and to unfasten the belt; the piece pooled on the ground next to the babydoll. "Now look at me and stand up straight," he directed. I gazed back at Louis, fully erect, slightly pigeon-toed, knees nearly touching, arms a bit behind my sides.

I was in a vulnerable pose and was indeed was feeling truly vulnerable. I was so deranged by an unrequited sexual frenzy that I had lost control of all my voluntary thoughts and movements. What I had intended as an act had turned into real submission to Louis.

"How considerate, Miss Wilder, you have left me with the opportunity to carefully inspect your legs and feet. You know how much I admire them ... and your delicate sandals, I find them so very sensual." He paused for a moment, just staring at me and now rubbing the bulge underneath his shorts. After a while, he continued, "Please lie back on that black leather chair over there. And spread your legs wide."

I did as he asked, stumbling and almost unconscious, as my brain was now a dense haze of fear and desire. After staring at my moaning and wanton form for a minute, Louis drew toward me and kneeled. He wrapped his hands around my ankles and buried his head in my crotch, his tongue alternating on my uncovered upper thighs, licking off the juices. My pussy now felt as if it was pouring out like a faucet and he responded by lapping up my slit over and over. At the top of each slurp, he pressed his tongue against my clit, each time eliciting a loud whimper that pierced through my otherwise non-stop moaning. He continued at this for an agonizing amount of time and I was starting to pass out. Just before I would have passed out, his lips locked in on my clit, sucking it hard while simultaneously inserting fingers inside me. I shuddered violently, felt a painful wave of pleasure, shrieked, and then went blank.

When I awoke, my stockings were off and I was lying sideways across the wide arms of the leather chair. Louis was smiling at me five feet away on his huge bed, lying nude halfway inside its sheets. "Would you like to come to bed now, Barb?"

I nodded and swung myself off the chair. I stood up, my sandals still apparently on. I slowly moved over toward the bed, knowing Louis was getting off on watching my naked body teetering in my sexy heels. Before I could lie down, Louis asked, "Could you take down your hair? I want to see you in your full glory."

"Anything, my dear," I replied. It took me over a minute to remove all the pins holding my updo in place. I shook my head and my long, voluminous hair draped over my entire upper body. I swept it back, uncovering a pleading smile directed at Louis. "Make love to me now, sweetie."

Louis motioned me to lie down and I did. He rolled me onto my back, between the warm and slippery satin sheets. Slowly and gently, his manhood penetrated me. His rock-hard penis felt so good and so natural inside me. It filled me up, both physically and spiritually. There was nothing to say. We gazed at each other, as he patiently went in and out of my sex, pausing every few strokes to tenderly kiss different parts my smiling face. After about fifteen minutes of mutual bliss, he whispered, "May I cum?"

I nodded adoringly. He thrust more quickly and I felt my pussy flooded. His eyes looked down at mine lovingly and I responded in kind. We embraced intimately, kissing deeply until his penis softened.

He pulled out and much of his seed spilled out onto the sheets. Neither one of us cared. I turned slightly to my right side, lying on some wetness. Louis did the same, his right arm under my neck and his left arm draped over the two large mounds on my chest.

He was tenderly spooning me and we dozed off in that position. I am so happy I have him all to myself. I felt fulfilled.

THE END